WORDS TO KNOW

ball

goal

kick

soccer

team

SIGHT WORDS

a
are
get
into
play
run
the
to
want
we
with

We play **soccer**.

CHILD

Soccer is a sport played on a field called a pitch.

ADULT

I READ! YOU READ!

Child's Turn to Read

Adult's Turn to Read

WE READ ABOUT SOCCER

by KIM THOMPSON and MADISON PARKER

TABLE OF CONTENTS

SEAHORSE PUBLISHING

Parent and Caregiver Guide

Reading aloud with your child has many benefits. It expands vocabulary, sparks discussion, and promotes an emotional bond. Research shows that children who have books read aloud to them have improved language skills, leading to greater school success.

I Read! You Read! books offer a fun and easy way to read with your child. Follow these guidelines.

Before Reading

- Look at the front and back covers. Discuss personal experiences that relate to the topic.
- Read the *Words to Know* on page 3. Talk about what the words mean.
- If the book will be challenging or unfamiliar to your child, read it aloud by yourself the first time. Then, invite your child to participate in a second reading.

During Reading

CHILD Have your child read the words beside this symbol. This text has been carefully matched to the reading and grade levels shown on the cover.

ADULT You read the words beside this symbol.

- Stop often to discuss what you are reading and to make sure your child understands.
- If your child struggles with decoding a word, help them sound it out. If it is still a challenge, say the word for your child and have them repeat it after you.
- To find the meaning of a word, look for clues in the surrounding words and pictures.

After Reading

- Praise your child's efforts. Notice how they have grown as a reader.
- Ask and answer questions about the book.
- Discuss what your child learned and what they liked or didn't like about the book.

Most importantly, let your child know that reading is fun and worthwhile. Keep reading together as your child's skills and confidence grow.

soccer

We want to get the **ball.** CHILD

You try to take the **ball** from the other team. ADULT

ball

We run with the ball.

CHILD

As you run with the ball, you dribble it between your feet.

ADULT

We **kick** the ball.

CHILD

You **kick** the ball with shoes called cleats.

ADULT

kick

We want to kick the ball into the **goal**.

CHILD

The team that kicks the ball into the **goal** scores one point.

ADULT

goal

We are a soccer **team**!

CHILD

A soccer **team** has players who play different positions.

ADULT

team

Index

Written by: Kim Thompson and Madison Parker
Design by: Jen Bowers
Series Development: James Earley

Photos: cover ©2010 Monkey Business Images/Shutterstock; p.5 ©2018 Fotokostic/Shutterstock; p.6 Vector-3D/Shutterstock; p.7 ©2018 Pressmaster/Shutterstock; p.8 ©2008 Rob Marmion/Shutterstock; p.9 ©2019 LightField Studios/Shutterstock, ©2014 Monkey Business Images/Shutterstock; p.10 ©2016 ETAP/Shutterstock, ©2016 Africa Studio/Shutterstock; p.11 ©2017 Fotokostic/Shutterstock; p.12 ©2017 Fotokostic/Shutterstock, ©2014 Monkey Business Images/Shutterstock; p.13 ©2020 kravik93/Shutterstock; p.15 ©2014 Brocreative/Shutterstock

Library of Congress PCN Data
We Read About Soccer / Kim Thompson and Madison Parker
I Read! You Read!
ISBN 979-8-8873-5190-2 (hard cover)
ISBN 979-8-8873-5210-7 (paperback)
ISBN 979-8-8873-5230-5 (EPUB)
ISBN 979-8-8873-5250-3 (eBook)
Library of Congress Control Number: 2022945526

Printed in China

Seahorse Publishing Company
www.seahorsepub.com

Published in the United States
Seahorse Publishing
PO Box 771325
Coral Springs, FL 33077

SEAHORSE PUBLISHING